The Case of the Runaway Dog

Read all the Jigsaw Jones Mysteries

Coming Soon

The Case of the Runaway Dog

by James Preller
illustrated by John Speirs
cover illustration by R. W. Alley

A
LITTLE APPLE
PAPERBACK

SCHOLASTIC INC.
New York Toronto London Auckland Sydney
Mexico City New Delhi Hong Kong

For Nicholas —

thanks for the great ideas!

J
Preller
10.14

Book design by Dawn Adelman

No part of this work may be reproduced, stored in a retrieval system, or transmitted in any form or by any means, electronic, mechanical, photocopying, recording, or otherwise, without written permission of the publisher. For information regarding permission, write to Scholastic Inc., Attention: Permissions Department, 555 Broadway, New York, NY 10012.

ISBN 0-439-11426-8

Text copyright © 1999 by James Preller. Cover illustration © 1999 by R. W. Alley. Interior illustrations © 1999 by Scholastic Inc. All rights reserved. Published by Scholastic Inc. SCHOLASTIC, APPLE PAPERBACKS, and associated logos are trademarks and/or registered trademarks of Scholastic Inc.

12 11 10 9 8 7 6 5 4 3 2 1   9/9 0 1 2 3 4/0

Printed in the U.S.A.   40
First Scholastic printing, November 1999

CONTENTS

Chapter One

Pilgrims and Turkeys

I sat in my tree-house office, doing a lot of nothing much.

But that's the life of a detective. It's not always a parade of glory. There are days when I just hang around the office, waiting for the next case to show up.

I slugged down another glass of grape juice and decided to call it a day. After a quick phone call to Ralphie Jordan, we headed to Lincoln Park with my dog, Rags. The sky was clear and blue. A couple of

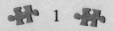

lonely clouds drifted by, looking like they were lost.

"Which is your favorite holiday?" Ralphie asked me as we walked into the park.

"Christmas," I answered.

Ralphie shrugged. "My family celebrates Kwanzaa, too."

"Do you get presents for Kwanzaa?"

"Sure," Ralphie replied. "But that's not what it's about. It's about celebrating our heritage."

I guess that was OK for Ralphie. Personally, I'd rather celebrate new toys. "How about this," I asked. "Which do you like better — Halloween or Valentine's Day?"

"Halloween," Ralphie answered. "More candy."

I agreed.

"How about Thanksgiving?" Ralphie asked.

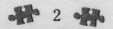 2

"I'm not crazy about the food," I complained.

"You know what bugs me about Thanksgiving?" Ralphie said, shaking his head. "Stuffing! I mean, what IS stuffing, anyway?"

"It's a mystery to me," I answered. "I'd rather have pizza any day." That settled it. When it came to holidays, Thanksgiving came in last place.

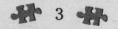 3

We stood in an open field. There was a big playground to our right. To our left was Long Hill — a big hill where we went sledding in the winter. And behind it was the lake.

Ralphie kicked a rock. "I have an idea," he said. "Let's pretend it's the first Thanksgiving. I'll be a Native American. You'll be a Pilgrim. And Rags can be the turkey!"

Rags looked up at us, alarmed. He didn't seem thrilled with the idea of playing a turkey. I couldn't blame him. After all, turkeys probably hate Thanksgiving. It's not exactly a terrific holiday when people eat you.

I let Rags off his leash. He was a good dog, in a slobbering kind of way. As usual, a string of drool dangled from his mouth. We pretended that our sticks were hatchets and chased Rags around the great lawn.

Suddenly, we saw Lucy Hiller, Mila Yeh, and Kim Lewis race past on Rollerblades. *Crash — kapowee!* They had a giant smack-up. All three of them were tangled in a knot. Ralphie and I raced over to make sure they were OK.

The girls were laughing like crazy hyenas. It was a good thing they wore helmets and pads. No one got hurt. After we talked for a while, I looked around and asked, "Hey, anybody see Rags?"

Chapter Two

The Search for Rags

"Here, Ragsy! Here, boy!"

"He's probably chasing a squirrel or something," Lucy offered. "My dog does it all the time."

I shook my head. "The only thing Rags chases is a free meal."

Ralphie frowned. "Maybe we shouldn't have been chasing him with sticks."

I put my hands to my mouth and bellowed, "Rags, come!"

Nothing.

Mila patted me on the back. She was my partner and best friend. "Don't worry, Jigsaw. He has to be around here someplace."

"What kind of dog is he again?" Kim asked.

"A Newfoundland," I said. "Gray and white. Just a big, hairy dog."

"Does he have a collar?"

"Yes," I answered. "And dog tags, too." That was the good news. If somebody found Rags, they could read our phone number and address on his tags.

We split up. Ralphie and I climbed the hill to search the trees. The girls did a loop around the park. On top of the hill, Ralphie and I could see in all directions. We saw a few people, but no dogs. "This isn't like Rags," I told Ralphie. "He'll wander sometimes. But Rags always comes back."

I pointed down toward the lake. "Let's see if anyone down there has seen him."

We talked to a man who was fishing from a rock. He hadn't seen anything. We talked to a lady with a baby. They were throwing bread into the water, feeding the ducks. They hadn't seen Rags, either.

"Maybe he wandered home," Ralphie suggested.

"That's across two streets!" I exclaimed. "Rags isn't allowed to cross the street by himself."

Now I was getting nervous. What if Rags *did* wander off? What if he got hit by a car? What if he . . . just . . . ran away?

"Rags!" I called out desperately. "Come on, boy!"

Ralphie pointed to a group of teenagers. "Hey, I know that girl. She lives across the street from me. That's Earl Bartholemew's sister, Carrie."

The teenagers were hanging out at the

edge of the lake. And they were doing what teenagers do best — just standing around, trying to look cool. Oh brother.

A girl with short black hair and a green jacket nodded hello. It was Carrie Bartholemew. "Hi there, Ralphie," she said, pushing him playfully. "Beautiful day, isn't it?"

"It used to be," Ralphie said, "until Jigsaw lost his dog."

Carrie looked at me and frowned. Carrie told us she hadn't seen any stray dogs. "We just got here," she explained.

Suddenly, Lucy Hiller, curly hair flying in the wind, called to us from the bicycle path.

"Jigsaw, come quick. Mila needs you."

Chapter Three

A Strange Witness

There's a boathouse at one end of the lake. In the summer, people go there to rent paddleboats. Then they set out on the lake — for an afternoon of sunburn and mosquito bites. Go figure.

The boathouse was closed for the fall. It would open again once sledding season began. That's because they made a fortune selling hot chocolate to frozen kids. Next to the boathouse, there was a garbage Dumpster. That's where we found Mila and Kim, standing awkwardly on Rollerblades.

They were talking to an old man dressed in an overcoat. He wore a scarf and a cap pulled tight over his head. He had an enormous nose that reminded me of a bird's beak. The man squinted at us.

"Jigsaw, this is Mr. Signorelli," Mila said. "He says he saw a dog that might have been Rags."

The old man reached out a yellowed hand and I shook it. "Pleased to meet you." His grip was surprisingly strong. He pulled

out a cigarette and lit it, coughing almost immediately. "I was just telling these young ladies that I did see something. Maybe it was your dog. Maybe not. My eyes ain't what they used to be."

Yeesh. A witness with bad eyes is like a polar bear wearing a purple tutu. Detectives don't have much use for them.

"I guess you could say this is my home away from home," he began. "Now that I'm retired, I spend most of my days in the park. I've made friends with a few squirrels. I bring 'em peanuts and we keep each other company. I don't know who looks forward to our visits more — me or them."

Mr. Signorelli took another deep drag of his cigarette. His eyes were red around the edges. And I noticed, for the first time, wisps of gray hair growing out of his ears.

"The dog," I reminded him. "You said you saw a dog."

"Pretty big one, too," he said. "Sniffing around by the Dumpster."

"Was he gray and white?" I asked.

Mr. Signorelli ran his fingers across his chin. A long, gray ash fell from his cigarette. "Maybe yes. Maybe no. With these eyes, I couldn't be sure one way or the other. But it was a big dog, I'll tell you that."

Mila coughed. "Mr. Signorelli, sir," she said. "Please tell him about the girl."

I shot a glance at Mila. "What girl?" I asked.

"Well, I *think* it was a girl," Mr. Signorelli said. "Hard to tell these days, ain't it? Boys wearing long hair and earrings and all. I can't keep track." He chuckled softly to himself. "Anyway, she was petting the dog. They seemed to be getting along pretty good."

"Did you notice anything else?" I asked.

Mr. Signorelli closed his eyes. For a minute, I almost thought he had fallen asleep. But he opened them suddenly and smiled.

"Pretzels," he said. "She was feeding him pretzels."

Chapter Four

Home Alone

When the sunlight touched the trees in the distance, I knew it was time to face my parents. They were going to kill me. The surprising thing was, I didn't even care. There was nothing they could say or do that would make me feel any worse.

We left the park empty-handed.

Lucy and Kim went home in the other direction. Heels dragging, I trudged between Ralphie and Mila. We stopped in front of Ralphie's house. "You okay?" he asked me.

I shook my head. "Nope."

Ralphie opened his mouth to speak. Maybe it was a joke or something to make me feel better. That would have been Ralphie's style. But he stopped short, turned, and ran inside the house. I guess he knew there was nothing to say.

Mila said good-bye, too. But I wasn't listening. All I could think about was Rags. He was out there somewhere. Maybe he was lost. Maybe he was hurt. I didn't know. I only knew that he was alone.

My family was already seated at the dinner table when I got home. "Where have you been?" my mother scolded.

But when she saw my face, her expression changed. "Theodore?" she said. "What is it?"

My father got up and walked toward me. "Son, are you all right? Where's Rags?"

It would have been easier if they yelled and screamed. But they didn't. My parents hugged me . . . and we talked . . . and they said everything was going to be all right.

"It's not your fault," my dad said. "It'll be okay. We'll find Ragsy, don't you worry."

My father threw on his coat and took my three brothers — Billy, Daniel, and Nicholas — in the station wagon. They went looking for Rags. My sister, Hillary, volunteered to call the animal hospital.

I felt a twinge in my stomach. "Animal hospital?" I asked.

My mother gave Hillary a look. "Just in case," my mother said. "I'm sure Rags is fine."

My mom tried to make me eat some macaroni and cheese. I took a few bites, but my heart wasn't in it. I went into my room and pulled out my detective journal. On a clean page I wrote: **THE CASE OF THE RUNAWAY DOG**. Usually, I loved mysteries. But that was when they happened to *other* people. This was *my* mystery — and it

wasn't any fun. I pulled out a jigsaw puzzle. It was a picture of cavemen battling a saber-toothed tiger. I gave up after a few minutes. None of the pieces seemed to fit. Finally, I crawled into bed and pulled the covers over my head.

Later, my father came home with my brothers. I could tell by their quiet voices that they'd come home alone. I rolled over in my empty bed. Rags was gone.

And it was all my fault.

Chapter Five

Room 201

On Monday, I wanted to stay home to help look for Rags. But my mother wouldn't listen. "You worry about school," she told me. "Rags will turn up."

"But . . ."

"But me no buts, Theodore," she said.

"But . . ."

Then she gave me . . . the look.

It meant: *End of discussion*.

Yeesh.

Mila sat next to me on the school bus.

Mila was usually singing a song, but not today. She was too busy thinking.

"What did you think of Mr. Signorelli?" she asked.

"I don't know," I answered. "He was kind of weird."

Mila shook her head. "Not weird," she said. "Lonely. There's a difference."

I thought about Mr. Signorelli. He did seem a little lonely, now that Mila mentioned it. He said the squirrels kept

him company. That's pretty bad, when squirrels are your pals. Maybe that's why he was so eager to talk with us. Mr. Signorelli didn't have anyone else.

"I'm too upset. I can't think straight," I told Mila.

"It's OK, Jigsaw," Mila said. "I'll help you find Rags."

Our class was in Room 201. We were lucky to have Ms. Gleason for a teacher. But I wasn't feeling very lucky. Or very thankful — which was too bad, since that was the topic of our homework assignment.

"Boys and girls," Ms. Gleason said, "Thanksgiving is in three days. You all know what that means."

Ralphie Jordan piped up, "Yeah, no school!"

Everybody cheered.

Ms. Gleason smiled. "Yes, we could all use a few days off." Then she told us about the first Thanksgiving. "Why were the Pilgrims thankful?" she asked.

"Because of the good harvest," Athena Lorenzo answered.

"That's right, Athena," Ms. Gleason said. "The pilgrims knew they had enough food for the long, hard winter ahead. They were thankful, so they had a big feast to celebrate."

Ms. Gleason stopped and looked at us. "Things are different today. We have supermarkets and restaurants and frozen TV dinners. Most of us aren't farmers. Why do we celebrate Thanksgiving now?"

No one had an answer. Mila slowly raised her hand. "To give thanks?" she asked.

Ms. Gleason smiled. "Yes, Mila. It's a day when we all give thanks."

Ms. Gleason wrote on the blackboard:

I AM THANKFUL FOR . . .

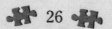 26

She continued, "On Wednesday, I'd like you to come in with a list of five things you are thankful for."

Bigs Maloney pumped his fist in the air. "Professional wrestling!"

"Sony PlayStation!" Eddie Becker called out.

Danika Starling protested, "You guys are all wrong. We're supposed to be thankful for important stuff." She cleared her throat. "I am thankful for . . . Beanie Babies!" Danika took a deep bow.

"That's very funny, Danika," Ms. Gleason said. "But there are no right or wrong answers to this homework assignment. The important thing is that you spend time thinking about it."

A few other kids spoke up. It seemed like everybody was thankful for something. But when Ms. Gleason called on me, my mind went blank. I couldn't think of anything.

Anything, that is, except for Rags. "I'm not feeling very thankful today," I mumbled.

Ms. Gleason made a face.

"Think harder," she told me. "We all have reasons to be thankful."

Oh brother. That was easy for Ms. Gleason to say.

Her dog wasn't missing.

Chapter Six

The Animal Rescue Shelter

Mila handed me a note at the end of the day. It was in code. She liked to test my brainpower. This time, she almost had me stumped.

24 * 11 33 * 22 35 24 34 22 * 12 11 13 31 * 45 35
* 32 35 35 31 * 21 35 43 * 33 35 43 15
* 13 32 51 15 44.

Then I remembered. It was called a checkerboard code. I pulled out my detective journal. First I drew a square with

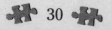

twenty-five boxes. Then I filled in the letters and numbered the rows and columns like this:

Column	1	2	3	4	5
Row 1	A	B	C	D	E
Row 2	F	G	H	I	J
Row 3	K	L	M	N	O
Row 4	P	Q	R	S	T
Row 5	U	V	W	X	Y/Z

To make the code, Mila changed each letter into a two-figure number. To make the letter *I*, for example, Mila wrote 24. The 2 stands for row 2. The 4 means column number 4. In another minute, I figured out the message. *I am going back to look for more clues.*

I looked up to see Mila smiling at me. I slid a finger across my nose. That was our secret signal. It meant I got the message.

When the bus dropped me off from school, the house was strangely quiet. No barks from behind the door. No happy dog jumping up to lick me. I usually hated it when Rags drooled on me. But today I would have given anything for a faceful of slime.

"Leave your coat on, detective," my oldest brother, Billy, called out. He came into the living room, twirling car keys around his finger. "We're going for a ride."

We drove steadily for about fifteen minutes. Billy pointed to a sign. "This is the place," he said.

The sign read: ANIMAL RESCUE SHELTER.

Billy winked. "You never know. We just might get lucky."

I'd never been to an animal shelter before. A very pretty girl with a long blond ponytail sat behind the counter. She had blue eyes and an earring in her nose. "Can I help you?" she asked.

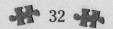 32

"We're looking for our dog," Billy explained. "He disappeared yesterday and we were wondering . . ."

"The dogs and cats are through that door," the girl said. "We get a few new animals every day. Feel free to take a look."

In the next room, the walls were lined with cages, stacked three high. There was a cat in nearly every cage. Some were calm and beautiful; others were skinny and skittish. But they all shared something in common. They didn't have a home.

The dogs were kept in another room. It was like a big garage, with a cement floor and cement walls. The dogs were locked behind high, narrow fences. Some dogs sat and stared as we walked past. A cute Dalmatian leaped against the fence, whining sadly. Most dogs barked. You didn't have to be Doctor Dolittle to

understand what they were saying —
"Take me, take me. I'll be good. Take me!"

Other dogs just lay on the ground beside their water bowls. They didn't seem to care one way or the other. They only lifted their heads and followed us with blank eyes.

It was one of the saddest places I'd ever been.

We didn't find Rags.

"Let's cut out of here," Billy said. "This place creeps me out."

On the way out, I asked the girl, "What happens to them?"

Her lips drew together tightly. "We never put them to sleep, if that's what you mean. This is a no-kill shelter. We hold on to our animals until someone adopts them."

"But what if no one . . . ?"

She looked steadily into my eyes. "We try to love them the best we can."

Billy dropped a handful of change into a donation box. "Thanks," he said. "You guys do good work."

And we left — the sound of barking still in our ears.

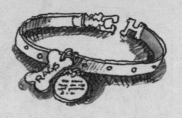

Chapter Seven

A Visit from Mila

There was a sharp knock on my bedroom door. Grams walked into my room before I could answer. I was lying on my bed, staring at the ceiling.

Grams turned on a lamp and opened the curtains. "It's too dark in here," she complained. "Why are you moping around, anyway?"

I sighed. Grams didn't understand. "There's no law against moping," I said.

"Around me there is," she snapped. "How are we going to get Rags back with

you lying in a dark room, feeling sorry for yourself? Come on, up and at 'em. We've got work to do."

She turned to leave the room. "And bring your markers," she demanded.

At the dining room table, Grams watched over my shoulder as I took out a large piece of paper. At the top, in big letters, I wrote the word MISSING! Below I drew a picture of Rags. "Looks just like him," Grams said approvingly. "Don't forget to include our phone number. I'll send your father to get copies made at Kinko's. It will be *your* job to put them up after school tomorrow."

I didn't hear the doorbell ring. That's because I was used to Rags. He was better than a doorbell, because he barked loudly when anyone came to the door.

"Your friends are here," my mom announced.

Mila came into the room. Kim Lewis, Lucy Hiller, and Ralphie Jordan followed.

"We went back to the park after school," Mila said. "We all wanted to help. Kim and Lucy found this."

Mila pulled a blue dog collar from her coat pocket. She handed it to me. I didn't need to read the dog tags. After all, I had picked it out myself.

"Where'd you find this?" I asked.

"Near the footbridge," Lucy answered.

"Maybe it came loose and fell off," Ralphie offered.

I didn't think so. The collar fit snugly on Rags. I checked to see if it was broken. The

collar snapped together easily. It was working just fine.

Mila pulled on her long black hair. "That leaves only one explanation," she said.

We all looked at her.

"Somebody took it off," Mila said.

She was right, of course. That was the only thing that could have happened.

Somebody took off his collar. But why?

I knew the answer immediately. But I didn't like it. Not one bit. They took off the collar because they didn't want Rags to be found.

He'd been dognapped.

Chapter Eight

The Green Thread

Something caught my eye. I looked closely at the collar. I carefully pulled off a green thread.

"What's that?" Kim asked.

I held the thread between my fingers. "This, my friends, is a clue. The dognapper may have been wearing green."

It was almost time for dinner. I walked my friends to the door. "See you, Jigsaw," Ralphie said.

As they started down the walk, I called

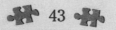

out to them. "Hey, guys," I said. "Listen, um, thanks — thanks a lot."

Grams was right. I was moping when I should have been hoping. Great detectives don't solve mysteries by lying around. They work. They examine clues. They visit the scene of the crime. They keep trying until the case is solved.

I ran to my bedroom and pulled out my journal. I listed the clues. Then I tried to think of suspects. I wrote down two:

 44

| 1. MR. SIGNORELLI |
| 2. THE MYSTERY GIRL |

Mr. Signorelli seemed nice enough. There was nothing about him that told me he was a dognapper. I remembered that his coat wasn't green. But the scarf . . .

It may have been green, or blue. I closed my eyes and tried to remember. What color was it? Could *he* have stolen Rags? Mr. Signorelli was lonely, I knew that much. He probably would have loved to have a dog to keep him company. I mean, a dog sure beats a lousy bunch of squirrels. Maybe he lied about seeing the girl.

I just couldn't be absolutely positive.

I telephoned Mila. She said Mr. Signorelli's scarf was red and yellow. "It couldn't have been Mr. Signorelli," she argued. "We saw him in the park when Rags disappeared. He was alone."

45

"Maybe," I said. "But anything is possible — and everyone's a suspect. I mean, how much do we *really* know about the guy? I'm going to have another chat with Mr. Signorelli tomorrow."

Mila paused on the phone. "I've been thinking about the girl with the pretzels," she said. "Rags likes pretzels, right?"

"Rags loves pretzels," I answered.

"Would Rags, maybe, follow someone . . . if they gave him pretzels?"

"He might," I said.

"We've got to find that girl," Mila concluded. "If Mr. Signorelli saw her in the park, maybe somebody else did, too."

"That's a big *if*," I replied. I reminded her that Mr. Signorelli's eyesight wasn't very good.

We reviewed the facts of the case. I told Mila about climbing the hill and going down to the lake. I told her about the man

on the rock and the mother and baby feeding bread to the ducks.

"Anything else?" Mila asked.

"Oh, yeah," I said. "There were some teenagers. One of them was Ralphie's neighbor, Carrie Bartholemew. But none of them saw anything."

"Were any of them wearing green?" Mila asked.

I pictured the teenagers in my mind. "Yes," I answered. "Carrie Bartholemew had short black hair . . . and a green wool jacket."

Chapter Nine

The Mystery Girl

I couldn't wait for school to end on Tuesday. "Remember your homework assignment," Ms. Gleason reminded us during cleanup. "I look forward to reading all the reasons why you feel thankful."

I eased over to her desk. "Excuse me, Ms. Gleason."

"Yes, Theodore?"

"Um, well, I can't do that assignment. Is there something else I can do instead?"

Ms. Gleason looked puzzled. "I don't understand," she said.

I told her about Rags. "It's kind of hard to be thankful when you feel rotten," I explained.

"I'm sorry about Rags," Ms. Gleason said. "But you still have to do the homework. Even when we're sad, we all have reasons to be thankful. And when we're feeling rotten, it's especially important to remember the good things in life." Ms. Gleason shoved folders into her bulging book bag.

Without looking up, she said, "I expect to see that homework on my desk tomorrow, Theodore."

Yeesh.

We met in front of my house after school. Nearly everybody was there — Lucy, Kim, Ralphie, and Mila. I handed out posters and tape. We split up. The neighborhood would be plastered with posters in no time. But first, I handed Ralphie a baggy with the green thread. "I have a special job for you," I told him. "Somehow, you've got to get ahold of Carrie Bartholemew. Check this thread against her jacket. See if it's a match."

Ralphie looked at me, surprised. "Do you think she did it?"

"I don't think anything," I answered. "I just follow the clues."

I began to feel a little better. At least I was *doing something*, instead of moping.

I thought about what Ms. Gleason said. I guess you could say I was . . . *thankful*.

It was nice to have good friends.

Mila and I rode our bicycles into the park to look for Mr. Signorelli. We found him by the picnic tables, sitting alone, surrounded by a handful of squirrels. Mr. Signorelli held a peanut in his hand. Slowly, cautiously, a squirrel moved closer, closer. Suddenly, it snatched the nut and scampered away. You should have seen the smile on Mr. Signorelli's face.

"This is a nice surprise," he said as we pedaled to a stop. "I was just thinking about that dog of yours. Any luck?"

We shook our heads.

Mr. Signorelli pulled out a cigarette and began to light it.

"You shouldn't smoke," I said.

He scowled. "You sound like my doctor."

"No, just a friend," I replied. "Besides,

you don't need to be a doctor to know that smoking is bad for your health."

Mr. Signorelli sighed and laid the unlit cigarette on the picnic table. I handed him the poster. He eyed it carefully, holding the poster at arm's length. "That's the dog, all right. I'm sure of it."

He suddenly snapped his fingers. "You know, I just saw that girl a few minutes ago." He pointed toward the lake. "She was walking toward the footbridge. If you hurry, you can catch up with her."

We were gone faster than you can say Peter Piper picked a peck of pickled peppers.

We reached her before she crossed the footbridge. "Excuse me," Mila called out sweetly. "I was wondering if you could help us?"

The girl looked at us. "Oh, I suppose," she said reluctantly.

She was tall. Red sweater, jeans. Dirty blond bangs fell over her eyes. I figured her for ten years old. Eleven, tops. Probably a fourth-grader.

Mila gave her the poster. She glanced at it quickly, then shoved the paper into her jeans pocket. "I don't like dogs," she said.

"But have you *seen* him?" Mila asked. "We lost him in the park."

"Nope, never saw him in my life," she answered quickly. "Besides, I just moved here. And I definitely wasn't in the park on Sunday."

"Is that so?" Mila said.

The girl blew air out of her mouth, making her bangs rise, then fall. "I was at the mall all day, shopping. Any more questions?" She turned to leave.

I was about to speak when Mila poked me in the ribs. "Let her go," Mila whispered.

"But . . ."

Mila shushed me.

We watched her cross over the bridge and walk toward the street.

"Come on," Mila said. "Let's follow her."

Chapter Ten

Proof!

We hung back as far as we could, while still keeping an eye on the girl with bangs. She crossed the street, turned right, then walked up a stone pathway and disappeared into a yellow house. I wrote the address in my journal: 41 **LAKEVIEW ROAD.**

"She knows something," Mila said. "All we need now is proof."

I was surprised. "What makes you so sure?" I asked.

Mila nodded, grim and determined. "She made a mistake," Mila said. "She told us *too much*. When people lie, sometimes they say more than they need to. Do you remember what she said when I told her we lost Rags?"

"She said she was at the mall all day," I answered.

Mila corrected me. "She also said: '*And I definitely wasn't in the park on Sunday.*'"

I grabbed Mila by the shoulders. "Of course, that's it! We never *told* her what day Rags was missing! How could she have known it was Sunday?"

Mila glanced at her watch. "There's still time," she said. "If we're right, Rags will be home with you . . . tonight."

On the way back to my house, Mila sang as she rode. That was a good sign. It meant she was happy. And Mila was happiest when we were solving a case. The tune was "London Bridge Is Falling Down." But Mila changed the words around:

"Ragsy is a drooling dog,
drooling dog, drooling dog,
Ragsy is a drooling dog.
Watch out you've been slimed!"

I called Ralphie Jordan right away. He told me the thread didn't match. "Thanks, Ralphie," I told him. "I just needed to be sure. Now I've got one more favor to ask. . . ."

We stashed our bikes behind some bushes and hid. Mila and I watched Ralphie walk up to the yellow house on 41 Lakeview Road. The girl with bangs answered the door. We couldn't hear what Ralphie was saying, but I had a pretty good idea.

See, we needed proof. But Mila and I couldn't be the ones to get it. The girl had already seen us. She knew we were looking for Rags. But Ralphie Jordan was a new face. We told him to knock on the door and say he was on a scavenger hunt. He was supposed to ask for a couple of usual things — a safety pin, a yellow pencil — and one very important item: a piece of thread from a green sweater.

In a few minutes, Ralphie was back, huffing and puffing. He held out the thread, his face beaming with pride.

It was a perfect match.

"She's the one," Mila said, gritting her teeth.

"There's something else," Ralphie added. "When I knocked on the door, I heard barking."

"What kind of barking?" I asked.

Ralphie made a face. "I dunno. Just . . . barking."

"Think, Ralphie," I said. "Was it a yip-yap type of bark? Or more of a woof-woof?"

Ralphie told me it was more of a woof-woof-type bark.

I stood up. "Wait here. I'm going to get Rags."

"Alone?" Mila asked.

"He's my dog," I answered. "My responsibility. I'm going alone."

Chapter Eleven

Family Reunion

All liars are afraid of one thing.

And that's The Truth.

Sure, at first she denied everything. But I had the facts. I had the proof. All the pieces fit together like a jigsaw puzzle. So I planted my feet, crossed my arms, and told her that I wasn't leaving without my dog. "Unless," I said, "you prefer I call the police."

Maybe she was lonely in her new neighborhood. Maybe she always wanted a good dog. Maybe when she saw Rags, she saw a chance to have a big, wonderful pet to love. It didn't matter to me, not really. Because Rags was mine.

She messed with the wrong guy.

"I told my parents he was a stray," she said, half apologizing. "I just wanted to love him. . . ."

"Save the excuses," I interrupted. "And meantime, try the Animal Rescue Shelter. They have dogs that really do need your love."

Getting home was the best part. Rags bounded into the house like a runaway bumper car. He jumped from person to person — leaping at my dad, wrestling with my brothers, licking my sister, Grams, and Mom. Then he jumped on me so hard, he knocked me to the floor. There I was, flat on my back, with Rags sitting on top of me. He licked me in the face over and over.

Being slimed never felt so good.

After things settled down, it was life as

usual in the Jones house. We were a family again. Complete, together. Grams watched her show on television. Billy went "out." Hillary chatted on the phone with friends. Daniel and Nicholas argued over the computer. And I did my homework, with Rags lying by my feet.

It turned out pretty well.

I AM THANKFUL FOR...
1. My family
2. My friends
3. My dog
4. Jigsaw puzzles
5. Mysteries

I found that I couldn't stop at five. I added all kinds of things:

6. Pizza
7. Grape juice

8. Holidays
9. Clues
10. Star Wars
11. Frozen mini-waffles
12. Legos
13. Room 201
14. The New York Mets

For some reason, I began to think about Mr. Signorelli. After all, he helped crack the case. I thought about him in the park, sitting alone at the picnic table.

And I had one last, wonderful idea.

Chapter Twelve

Thanksgiving

It was Thanksgiving morning. My mom and dad were busy making the turkey, with help from Grams and Hillary. My brothers went out to play football in the park.

"Come on, Worm," Nicholas invited. "We could use you."

I told them I had something better to do.

After an hour, I almost gave up. But finally he came, as I knew he would.

"Well, hello there, young fella," Mr. Signorelli said. He sat down at the picnic table opposite me. "I see you found your dog."

"Thanks to you," I said.

"Wasn't nothing," he replied. Then Mr. Signorelli made a clicking sound with his tongue — *tcch, tcch*. In a moment, a few squirrels drew near. But this time they held back, fearful.

"It's your dog," he said, patting Rags on the head. "The squirrels are nervous with him around."

I held the leash tight. "Um, Mr. Signorelli?"

The old man looked at me, waiting.

"What are you doing today? For Thanksgiving, I mean."

He scratched the end of his nose and looked out across the lake. I followed his gaze. But there was nothing there. Just water and emptiness.

He shrugged. "Probably pop a TV dinner in the oven and watch the football games."

"No family?" I asked.

"Kids have grown up, moved away," he explained. "My wife, Sophia, well, she passed on a few years ago."

He looked into the sky, as if searching for a bird that wasn't there.

"You're not smoking today," I noticed.

Mr. Signorelli waved his hand, like swatting away a pesky fly. "Don't make a big deal out of it," he said. "I'm not making any promises. Maybe I'll quit. Maybe I won't. We'll see what happens."

It was now or never. I took a deep breath and talked fast. "We have a great TV. It's perfect for watching football games. And my sister and brothers are nice, most times. I'm sure they'll be nice today, because it's a holiday and they have to. The thing is, I told my parents about you, Mr. Signorelli. They're grateful for your help. . . ."

I was making a mess of it. He didn't understand.

"It's just that . . . well . . . my parents said it's OK and even Grams said it sounded like a terrific idea."

Mr. Signorelli tugged at his coat sleeves. He looked at me questioningly.

Finally I blurted it out. "Would you like to come to our house? For Thanksgiving dinner, I mean. Or maybe just dessert and coffee? My mom makes great pecan pie. You like coffee, don't you, Mr. Signorelli?"

Mr. Signorelli lifted his chin and peered at me over his enormous nose. I watched his eyes flicker, then decide. He reached into his pocket and, with a sweep of his arm, tossed a handful of peanuts to the squirrels. "Happy Thanksgiving, fellas!" he called out to them.

Then he stood up and rubbed his hands across his stomach. "I haven't had pecan pie in years." Mr. Signorelli smiled,

chuckling softly to himself. "You know what? I don't even remember your name."

"Jones," I answered. "Jigsaw Jones."

We walked out of the park together.

Just an old man, a dog on a leash, and me.

"Happy Thanksgiving, Mr. Signorelli," I said.

"Yes, it is," he said. "It really is."

He placed his hand on my shoulder. "Now tell me, Mr. Jones, about this Grams you mentioned. . . ."

My eyes darted up to Mr. Signorelli. He grinned and winked. I had to laugh.

Well, the case was over. I'd solved another mystery — thanks to Mila, my friends, and a kind stranger with hair growing out of his ears.

Go figure.

Maybe Thanksgiving wasn't such a bad holiday after all.